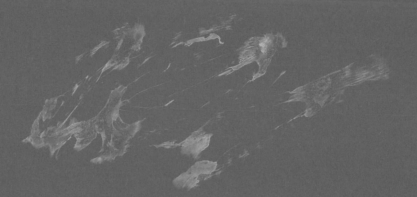

GALWAY COUNTY LIBRARIES

MOTHER & CHILD TREASURY

Selected by

SHIRLEY HUGHES

Illustrated by

CLARA VULLIAMY

TED SMART

CONTENTS

5356,139
£4.99.

INTRODUCTION

Sharing a story is one of the great pleasures of early childhood for parent and child alike. In putting together this plum-pudding mix of stories, I have been luckier with my illustrator than I ever dreamed at the outset. Not only was she once the child with whom I shared so many of them, but she herself is now doing the same thing with her own young family.

After the baby stage, when all the much-loved, well-thumbed picture books have been read over and over and satisfyingly digested, there comes the wonderful moment when you are ready for a 'proper' storybook. The wilder shores of fantasy being perhaps not yet quite negotiable, the essential stepping stone at this point is a story about believable real-life characters, a boy or girl 'just like me'. Reading aloud is so much a shared experience. Children love commenting, savouring the jokes (visual as well as verbal), and interjecting their own reactions to the plot. They are intent on the story but use it to reinforce and enhance their own experience of life. I suppose this is what all readers are doing, but at this stage it happens out loud. A delightful dialogue develops, one which neither Clara nor I, along with every other parent or carer, would miss for the world. And remembering our own pleasure in the countless re-readings of the doings of Milly-Molly-Mandy and Ameliaranne Stiggins and living them over again, combined with some great stories which have been written since and relished by my grandchildren, is how this collection came about.

Today, of course, it would naturally be as appropriate to put together a Father and Child Treasury. (Perhaps one day we will.) In trawling through traditional folk tales, I found to my surprise that mothers were rather sparsely represented. Wicked stepmothers galore, grandmothers too, but mothers tend either to die in the first paragraph or to exist as cross, warning characters on the sidelines of the narrative. Poor Mrs Stiggins, Constance Heward's overworked washerwoman, and Anne Fine's equally overstretched G. P. in *Poor Monty* are poles apart. But children, from their own viewpoint, will find both easily recognisable. A. A. Milne's elegant, leisured 1920's mother in her golden gown perhaps less so, but the bossy, proprietorial tone of her three-year-old son never fails to hit the spot.

Writers as diverse in style as Dorothy Edwards, Margaret Mahy, Allan Ahlberg and Philippa Pearce, internationally acclaimed as they are, are all mining an imaginative bedrock which underpins lasting children's fiction. The durability of their work stands out distinctively against some of the more ephemeral and thinly spread storylines of the ever-hungry media. Clara's illustrations are essential to forging this collection into a satisfying whole, not only as a joy to be pored over but as an integral part of each of these varied stories. With a lot of skilled help from our publishers, each spread is carefully designed to carry through the narrative. And the verses, whether they be by Colin McNaughton, Roald Dahl, A. A. Milne or Anon, she has relished using as a springboard for all sorts of characters and sub-plots of her own.

Editing this collection has been an entirely new experience for me and a highly illuminating one. I have had great pleasure in doing it. Most of all I am grateful to the authors, living or dead, for giving such lasting pleasures and for being permitted to offer some of them here.

Shirley Hughes

For Mark, Jack and Martha, with love.

MONDAY'S CHILD
IS RED AND SPOTTY

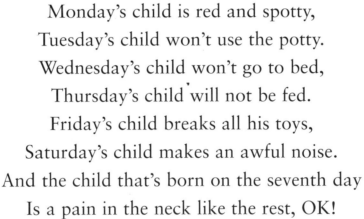

Monday's child is red and spotty,
Tuesday's child won't use the potty.
Wednesday's child won't go to bed,
Thursday's child will not be fed.
Friday's child breaks all his toys,
Saturday's child makes an awful noise.
And the child that's born on the seventh day
Is a pain in the neck like the rest, OK!

Colin McNaughton

My mother said that I never should
Play with the gypsies in the wood.
The wood was dark, the grass was green;
In came Sally with a tambourine.
Alpaca frock, new scarf-shawl,
White straw bonnet and a pink parasol.
I went to the river – no ship to get across,
I paid ten shillings for a blind white horse;
I up on his back and was off in a crack,
Sally tell my mother I shall never come back.

Traditional

Eight o'clock is striking,
Mother may I go out?
My young man is waiting
To take me round about.

First he gave me apples,
Then he gave me pears;
Then he gave me sixpence
To kiss him on the stairs.

Traditional (passed on from word
of mouth to Brian Alderson by his mum)

"Mother, may I have a swim?"
"Yes, my darling daughter.
Hang your clothes on yonder tree
But don't go near the water!"

Traditional

THE LITTLE GIRL AND THE TINY DOLL

by Aingelda Ardizonne

There was once a tiny doll who belonged to a girl who did not care for dolls.

For a long time she lay forgotten in a mackintosh pocket until one rainy day when the girl was out shopping.

The girl was following her mother round a grocer's shop when she put her hand in her pocket and felt something hard.

She took it out and saw it was the doll. "Ugly old thing," she said and quickly put it back again, as she thought, into her pocket.

But, in fact, since she didn't want the doll, she dropped it unnoticed into the deep freeze among the frozen peas.

The tiny doll lay quite still for a long time, wondering what was to become of her. She felt so sad, partly because she did not like being called ugly and partly because she was lost.

It was very cold in the deep freeze and the tiny doll began to feel rather stiff, so she decided to walk about and have a good look at the place. The floor was crisp and white, just like frost on a winter's morning. There were many packets of peas piled one on top of the other. They seemed to her like great big buildings. The cracks between the piles were rather like narrow streets.

She walked one way and then the other, passing, not only packets of peas, but packets of sliced beans, spinach, broccoli and mixed vegetables. Then she turned a corner and found herself among beef rissoles and fish fingers. However, she did not stop but went on exploring until she came to boxes of strawberries; and then ice cream.

The strawberries reminded her of the time when she was lost once before among the strawberry plants in a garden. Then she sat all day in the sun smelling and eating strawberries.

Now she made herself as comfortable as possible among the boxes.

The only trouble was that people were continually taking boxes out to buy them and the shop people were always putting in new ones.

At times it was very frightening. Once she was nearly squashed by a box of fish fingers.

The tiny doll had no idea how long she spent in the deep freeze. Sometimes it seemed very quiet. This, she supposed, was when the shop was closed for the night.

She could not keep count of the days.

One day when she was busy eating ice cream out of a packet, she suddenly looked up and saw a little girl she had never seen before. The little girl was sorry for the tiny doll and wished she could take her home.

The doll looked so cold and lonely, but the girl did not dare to pick her up because she had been told not to touch things in the shop. However, she felt she must do something to help the doll and as soon as she got home she set to work to make her some warm clothes.

First of all, she made her a warm bonnet out of a piece of red flannel.

This was a nice and easy thing to start with.

After tea that day she asked her mother to help her cut out a coat from a piece of blue velvet.

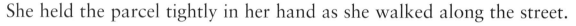

She stitched away so hard that she had just time to finish it before she went to bed. It was very beautiful.

The next day her mother said they were going shopping, so the little girl put the coat and bonnet in an empty match box and tied it into a neat parcel with brown paper and string.

She held the parcel tightly in her hand as she walked along the street.

As soon as she reached the shop she ran straight to the deep freeze to look for the tiny doll.

At first she could not see her anywhere. Then, suddenly, she saw her, right at the back, playing with the peas. The tiny doll was throwing them into the air and hitting them with an ice cream spoon.

The little girl threw in the parcel and the doll at once started to untie it. She looked very pleased when she saw what was inside.

She tried on the coat, and it fitted. She
tried on the bonnet and it fitted too.

She jumped up and down with
excitement and waved to the little girl
to say thank you.

She felt so much much better in
warm clothes and it made her feel happy
to think that somebody cared for her.

Then she had an idea. She made the
match box into a bed and pretended that
the brown paper was a great big blanket.
With a string she wove a mat to go
beside the bed.

At last she settled down in the match box, wrapped herself in the
brown paper blanket and went to sleep.

She had a long, long sleep because she was very tired and, when she
woke up, she found that the little girl had been back again and had left
another parcel. This time it contained a yellow scarf.

Now the little girl came back to the shop every day and each time she
brought something new for the tiny doll. She made her a sweater, a
petticoat, knickers with tiny frills, and gave her a little bit of a looking-
glass to see herself in.

She also gave her some red tights which belonged to one of her own
dolls to see if they would fit. They fitted perfectly.

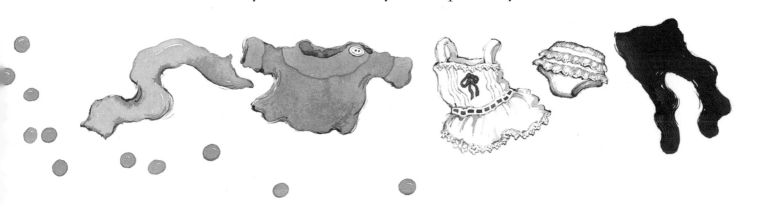

At last the tiny doll was beautifully dressed and looked quite cheerful, but still nobody except the little girl ever noticed her.

"Couldn't we ask someone about the doll?" the little girl asked her mother. "I would love to take her home to play with."

The mother said she would ask the lady at the cash desk when they went to pay for their shopping.

"Do you know about the doll in the deep freeze?"

"No indeed," the lady replied. "There are no dolls in this shop."

"Oh yes there are," said the little girl and her mother, both at once. So the lady from the cash desk, the little girl and her mother all marched off to have a look. And there, sure enough, was the tiny doll down among the frozen peas.

"It's not much of a life for a doll in there," said the shop lady, picking up the doll and giving it to the little girl. "You had better take her home where she will be out of mischief."

Having said this, she marched back to her desk with rather a haughty expression.

The little girl took the tiny doll home, where she lived for many happy years in a beautiful doll's house. The little girl played with her a great deal, but best of all the tiny doll liked the company of the other dolls. They all loved to listen to her adventures in the deep freeze.

KEITH'S CUPBOARD

Have you looked in Keith's cupboard?
You ought to.
You've never seen anything like Keith's cupboard.
Let's go over to Keith's place
and look in Keith's cupboard.

So when you get to Keith's place
you say,
"Can we play with your garage?"
And he says,
"No."
So you say,
"Can we play in your tent?"
And he says,
"No."
So you say,
"Can we play with your crane?"
And he says,
"No."

So you go up to Keith's mum
and you say,
"Can we play in Keith's tent?"
And she says,
"Keith, Keith,
why don't you get the tent out?"

"OK,"
says Keith,
and he starts going over to the cupboard –
Keith's cupboard.
He opens it, and –
Phew!

You've never seen anything like
Keith's cupboard.
In it
there's trucks, and garages, and tents
and cranes and forts and bikes and puppets
and games, and models and superhero suits
and hats and
he never plays with any of it.

They keep buying him all this stuff
and he never plays with it.

Day after day after day
it all sits in Keith's cupboard.

You ought to go over his place sometime
and have a look.
Keith's cupboard.
Phew!

Michael Rosen

THE SPECIAL OFFER PENS

from JOE AND TIMOTHY TOGETHER
by Dorothy Edwards

All the ladies who live in the tall, tall house in the big town like Special Offers. If a thing in a shop is called a Special Offer they always buy it, and if something in the paper is called a Special Offer and one of the ladies sends for it, all the other ladies send for it too, as soon as they have seen what it looks like.

So one day when the milkman who serves all the people in the tall house came along with a Special Offer of coloured pens, all the tall house ladies decided to have extra milk for a time so they could have the Special Offer pens.

Timothy's Mum got her pens first because of course they always need extra milk for the baby and for Timothy's Dad who likes it for his supper. But it wasn't long before Joe's and Jessie's mother got their pens too, and of course as Joe's and Timothy's and Jessie's Mums didn't need the pens for themselves they gave them to Joe and Timothy and Jessie to play with. (Jessie's brother Rupert who went to school wanted his Mum's pens too, and he made a fuss because they had been given to Jessie, but kind Miss Smithers gave her pens to Rupert because when she got them, she found that she didn't really need them.)

Anyway, each of the three friends had a box of coloured pens.

Now, as soon as Joe and Timothy got their Special Offer pens they tried them out at once to see what they wrote like.

Joe tried his pens out on the bottom of his Dad's newspaper because he knew Timothy had got into trouble trying *his* pens out on the gas bill, and of course, as soon as they had tried them out and seen how pretty they were they wanted to begin drawing with them.

Jessie's brother Rupert tried his pens out too, and Jessie watched him. Rupert used his pens to colour some black and white pictures in a comic. Jessie watched Rupert using his Special Offer pens, but she didn't try out her pens at all.

When Joe's Mum went down to pay for the papers, she bought Joe a big drawing-book with white pages to use his pens on; and Timothy's father gave him some wallpaper that had been left over when he had papered the bedroom, and the two little boys had a lovely time drawing things with their Special Offer pens.

Joe drew little tiny pictures in his big drawing-book. He drew little tiny trains, and cars and lorries and tractors, and tiny-tiny people. He sat at the table in his upstairs home among the chimney-pots and drew and drew, very, very slowly. He drew such tiny pictures that there were lots of pictures on each page of his book. All the time he was drawing he popped his tongue in and out.

When Joe's father saw Joe's drawings he said, "Well, well! I used to draw like that when I was little," and Joe's Mum said, "Yes, and you still pop your tongue in and out when you are concentrating hard." And they both laughed.

Timothy unrolled a lot of wallpaper on to his bedroom floor to make his drawing. Timothy doesn't draw little pictures like Joe's. He draws big pictures, and the picture he drew with his Special Offer pens was enormous.

Timothy drew a big, long picture. He drew a picture of the Park. He drew trees with green and brown pens and fountains with mauve and blue pens, and people playing tennis and pushing prams and sitting on seats and children swinging on swings with all the pens, one after the other. He drew the Special Lady in her yellow dress with the green dots on it. He drew Joe in his red trousers and Jessie with yellow bows on her hair. He drew the Park keeper and all the flowers. He drew birds eating crumbs and ducks eating crusts, and all the time Timothy drew he talked to himself. He said things like, "There, Special Lady! That's you running because you are late!" And, "That's you done, Duck. Now here is a brown crust for you!"

2356,139

Sometimes Timothy stopped drawing and went off to play "peep-bo" with Dawn Gloria, his tiny baby sister, and make her laugh. Sometimes he went out to the back yard to say "hello" to Alfie the cat, but afterwards he always went back and drew a bit more of his Park Picture. *His* Mum said, "One of these days you'll be a real artist if you go on like that!"

When Timothy couldn't get anything more on to his picture he asked his Mum to roll it up for him so that he could take it upstairs to show his friend Joe.

He carried his rolled-up picture very carefully all the way upstairs, and when he got to the landing where Jessie lived and saw her sitting outside her door playing with her dollie he said, "I'm going to show Joe my picture, Jessie. Would you like to see it too?"

Jessie said she would like to see it very much and Timothy said, "There's lots of room for it here. You unroll it for me, Jessie, while I go and fetch Joe."

So while Timothy went up to fetch Joe, Jessie unrolled the wallpaper picture, and when Joe and Timothy came down again she had laid it out flat on the landing, and to stop it curling up she had put her dollie on one end of it, and her little toy shopping-basket on the other end. Jessie is a very sensible child.

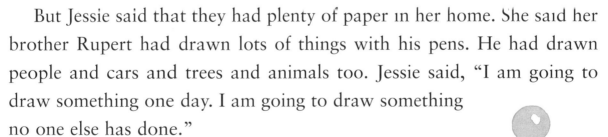

Joe had brought his drawing-book down to
show Timothy and Jessie his pictures. They had a
lovely time.

Joe and Jessie thought Timothy's Park
Picture was very nice. They were pleased
to see themselves in it and they recognised
the Special Lady at once. "You are a clever
boy, Timothy," Jessie said.

Then Jessie and Timothy looked at Joe's book,
at all the tiny tidy pictures. They thought they were very
interesting. Jessie said Joe was a clever boy too. She said,
"You can see which are engines and which are cars, Joe. I think
that it is very good."

Then Timothy said, "But haven't you drawn anything with your pens,
Jessie?" and Jessie said, "No, not yet."

Joe said, "Haven't you any paper? I'll tear the middle out of my
drawing-book for you if you like."

And Timothy said, "I've got lots more wallpaper downstairs,
Jessie. You can have some of that."

But Jessie said that they had plenty of paper in her home. She said her
brother Rupert had drawn lots of things with his pens. He had drawn
people and cars and trees and animals too. Jessie said, "I am going to
draw something one day. I am going to draw something
no one else has done."

And so she did. For one day, when her brothers Rupert
and Philip came home from school they were sucking some
very big round sweets. I expect you know the sort of sweets
I mean. When you suck them hard they get smaller, and as they
get smaller they change colour. Sometimes they are yellow,

sometimes brown, sometimes green and sometimes red and sometimes blue and sometimes mauve. Jessie's brothers kept taking them out of their mouths to see what colour they had changed to. They did this until their mother saw them and told them they were to throw them away at once.

Well now, Jessie went away into a corner. She took a piece of paper and she opened her box of Special Offer pens.

First she drew a black circle. "That's the outside," she said.

Then inside the black circle she drew a red circle, and inside that an orange circle, and inside the orange circle she drew a yellow circle, and inside the yellow circle she drew a green circle, and inside the green circle she drew a blue one and inside the blue one she made a mauve one, and there was just room to fill in the very middle with a big brown dot.

"Look everybody," Jessie said, "I've drawn a gob-stopper!" And she ran outside and went to look for Joe and Timothy to show them her picture.

BULLY BOY McCOY

I'm Bully Boy McCoy, ahoy!
An' bein' a bully's what I enjoy!
    I'll bully thee,
    If yer smaller'n me,
I'm Bully Boy McCoy, ahoy!

I'm Bully Boy McCoy, avast!
Hand o'er yer treasure an' make it fast!
    I'm hard as nails,
    I never fails!
I'm Bully Boy McCoy, avast!

I'm Bully Boy McCoy, ooh-arrgh!
I navigates by sun an' by star.
    An' stealin' treasure?
    That's me pleasure!
I'm Bully Boy McCoy, ooh-arrgh!

I'm Bully Boy McCoy, I be!
    I'm sailing home to have me tea.
    I'm in a state,
    Cos if I'm late –
My mummy will be cross with me!

Colin McNaughton

MASTER SALT THE SAILORS' SON

by Allan Ahlberg

Mr Salt the sailor sailed the seven seas.
Mrs Salt sailed the seven seas as well.
So did Miss Salt.
Master Salt did not sail the seas.
He was too little.
He stayed on shore with his grandpa.
One day exciting things happened.
Mr and Mrs Salt got ready for a voyage.
"We are going to sail to
Coconut Island," they said.
Their ship was called the *Jolly Jack*.
Mr Salt cleaned the cabins
and washed the deck.
Mrs Salt and Sally Salt painted the funnel.
Sammy Salt sulked.
He wanted to go on a voyage too.
The next day the *Jolly Jack*
was ready to sail.

Mr and Mrs Salt pulled up the anchor.

Grandpa Salt stood on the shore.

But where was Sammy Salt?

The *Jolly Jack* sailed out to sea.

Sally Salt blew a kiss to her grandpa.

He waved goodbye from the shore.

But *where* was Sammy Salt?

The voyage began.

The *Jolly Jack* sailed past a lighthouse.

Sally Salt got the dinner ready.

Somebody's little hand reached out.

"Who's been eating *my* fish?" said Mr Salt.

The *Jolly Jack* sailed past a big ship.

Mr Salt got the tea ready.

Somebody's little hand reached out again.

"Who's been eating *my* boiled egg?"

said Mrs Salt.

The *Jolly Jack* sailed past a whale.

Mrs Salt got the supper ready.

Somebody's little hand reached out again!

"Who's been drinking *my* cocoa?"

said Sally Salt.

In the night strange things happened.

Sally Salt woke up.

She said her nose kept tickling.

"Don't be silly, Sally," said Mr Salt.

Then Mr Salt went to bed and *he* woke up.

"My nose keeps tickling," he said.

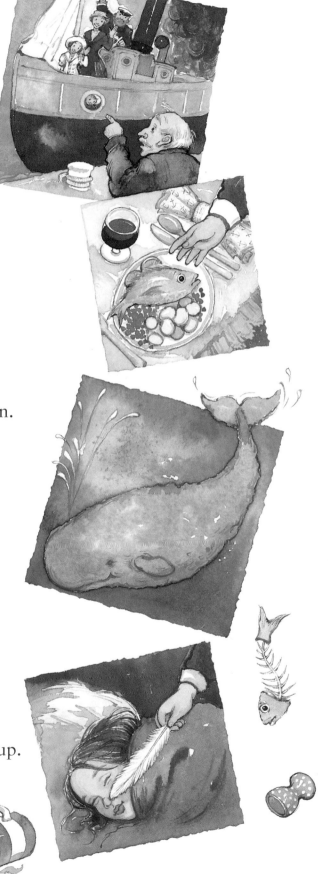

In the morning more strange things happened.
Somebody's little footprints appeared on deck.
Somebody's little teeth-marks
appeared in an apple.
When Mr Salt was fishing,
somebody's little boot appeared
on the end of his line.
Then, in the afternoon,
terrible things happened.
There was a storm.
The rain fell and the wind blew.
The thunder thundered and
the lightning flashed.
The *Jolly Jack* tipped up and down
– and Mr Salt fell overboard!
"MAN OVERBOARD!"
shouted Mr Salt.

Mrs Salt came to the rescue.
But still the *Jolly Jack* tipped up
and down – and *she* fell overboard!
"WOMAN OVERBOARD!"
shouted Mrs Salt.
Sally Salt came to the rescue.
But still the *Jolly Jack* tipped up
and down – and *she* fell overboard!
"GIRL OVERBOARD!"
shouted Sally Salt.
The next minute surprising things happened.
Somebody appeared on deck.
He threw a rope to Mr Salt.
"That's clever!" said Mr Salt.
He threw a lifebelt to Mrs Salt.
"Just what I need!" Mrs Salt said.
He threw a rubber-ring to Sally Salt.
She did not say a word.
He rescued them all!

"What a surprise!" said Mrs Salt.

"Look who it is!" said Mr Salt.

"Its Sammy!" said Sally.

Sammy Salt made hot drinks for his family.

He wrapped them up in blankets.

He steered the ship.

"Now I know who tickled my nose," said Mr Salt.

"And drank my cocoa," said Sally Salt.

"And ate my boiled egg!" Mrs Salt said.

"That's right," said Sammy Salt. "It was me!"

After that the best things happened.

The storm blew away.

The *Jolly Jack* reached Coconut Island.

There was a picnic on the shore,
and paddling in the sea,
and hide-and-seek in the jungle.
Bedtime came.
Mr and Mrs Salt and the children
slept out under the stars.
Then, in the night,
the last thing happened.
Sammy Salt woke up.
"My nose keeps tickling," he said.

DISOBEDIENCE

James James
Morrison Morrison
Weatherby George Dupree
Took great
Care of his Mother,
Though he was only three.
James James
Said to his Mother,
"Mother," he said, said he;
"You must never go down to the end of the town, if
   you don't go down with me."

James James
Morrison's Mother
Put on a golden gown,
James James
Morrison's Mother
Drove to the end of the town.
James James
Morrison's Mother
Said to herself, said she:
"I can get right down to the end of the town and be
   back in time for tea."

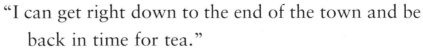

King John
Put up a notice,

LOST or STOLEN or STRAYED!

JAMES JAMES

MORRISON'S MOTHER

SEEMS TO HAVE BEEN MISLAID.

LAST SEEN

WANDERING VAGUELY:

QUITE OF HER OWN ACCORD,

SHE TRIED TO GET DOWN TO THE END OF THE

TOWN – FORTY SHILLINGS REWARD!

James James
Morrison Morrison
(Commonly known as Jim)
Told his
Other relations
Not to go blaming *him*.
James James
Said to his Mother,
"Mother," he said, said he:
"You must *never* go down to the end of the town without
consulting me."

James James
Morrison's Mother
Hasn't been heard of since.
King John
Said he was sorry,
So did the Queen and Prince.
King John
(Somebody told me)
Said to a man he knew:
"If people go down to the end of the town, well, what
can *anyone do*?"

(*Now then, very softly*)
J. J.
M. M.
W. G. Du P.
Took great
C/o his M*****
Though he was only 3.
J. J.
Said to his M*****
"M*****," he said, said he:
"You-must-never-go-down-to-the-end-of-the-town-if-
you-don't-go-down-with ME!"

A. A. Milne

AUNT NASTY

by Margaret Mahy

"Oh dear!" said Mother, one lunch time, after she had read a letter the postman had just left.

"What's the matter?" asked Father. Even Toby and Claire looked up from their boiled eggs.

"Aunt Nasty has written to say she is coming to stay with us," said Mother. "The thought of it makes me worried."

"You must tell her we will be out!" cried Toby. He did not like the sound of Aunt Nasty.

"Or say we have no room," said Father.

"You know I can't do that," said Mother. "Remember Aunt Nasty is a *witch*."

Toby and Claire looked at each other with round eyes. They had forgotten, for a moment, that Aunt Nasty was a witch as well as being an aunt. If they said there was no room in the house Aunt Nasty might be very cross. She might turn them into frogs.

"She is coming on the Viscount tomorrow," said Mother, looking at the letter. "It is hard to read this witch-writing. She writes it with a magpie's feather and all the letters look like broomsticks."

"I see she has written it on mouse skin," said Father.

"Isn't she just showing off?" asked Toby. "If she was a real witch she would ride a broomstick here... not come on the Viscount."

Claire had to move into Toby's room so that Aunt Nasty would have a bedroom all to herself. She put a vase of flowers in the room, but they were not garden flowers. Aunt Nasty liked flowers of a poisonous kind, like woody nightshade and foxgloves.

"Leave the cobwebs in that corner," said Father. "Remember how cross she was when you swept them down last time. She loves dust and cobwebs. All witches do."

The next afternoon they went to the airport to meet Aunt Nasty. It was easy to see her in the crowd getting off the Viscount. She was one of the old sort of witch, all in black with a pointed hat and a broomstick.

"Hello, Aunt Nasty," said Mother. "How nice to see you again."

"I don't suppose you are really pleased to see me," said
Aunt Nasty, "but that doesn't matter. There is a special
meeting of witches in the city this week. That is why
I had to come. I will be out every night on my
broom, and trying to sleep during the day.
I hope the children are quiet."

"Why didn't you come on your
broom, Aunt Nasty?" asked Toby. "Why
did you have to come in the aeroplane?"

"Don't you ever listen to the weather
report on the radio?" said Aunt Nasty
crossly. "It said there would be fresh
winds in the Cook Strait area,
increasing to gale force at midday. It
isn't much fun riding a broomstick in
a fresh wind let me tell you. Even the
silly aeroplane bucked around. I
began to think they'd put us into a
wheelbarrow by mistake. Two
people were sick."

"Poor people," said Claire.

"Serve them right!" Aunt
Nasty muttered. "People
with weak stomachs annoy
me."

When they got home
Aunt Nasty went straight
to her room. She smiled

at the sight of the foxgloves and the woody nightshade, but she did not say thank you.

"I will have a cat-nap," she said, stroking the raggy black fur collar she wore. "I hope the bed is not damp or lumpy. I used to enjoy a damp bed when I was a young witch, but I'm getting old now."

Then she shut the door. They heard her put her suitcase against it.

"What a rude aunt!" said Toby.

"She has to be rude, because of being a witch," said Mother. "Now, do be nice quiet children, won't you! Don't make her cross or she might turn you into tadpoles."

The children went out to play, but they were not happy.

"I don't like Aunt Nasty," said Claire.

"I don't like having a witch in the house," said Toby.

The house was very very quiet and strange while Aunt Nasty was there. Everyone spoke in whispery voices and went around on tiptoe. Aunt Nasty stayed in her room most of the time. Once she came out of her room and asked for some toadstools. Toby found some for her under a pine tree at the top of the hill... fine red ones with spots, but Aunt Nasty was not pleased with them.

"These are dreadful toadstools," she said. "They look good but they are quite disappointing. The brown, slimy ones are much better. You can't trust a boy to do anything properly these days. But I suppose I will have to make do with them."

That was on Tuesday. Some smoke came out of the keyhole on Wednesday, and on Thursday Aunt Nasty broke a soup plate. However, they did not see her again until Friday. Then she came out and complained that there was not enough pepper in the soup.

At last it was Sunday. Aunt Nasty had been there a week. Now she was going home again – this time by broomstick. Toby and Claire were very pleased. Mother was pleased too, and yet she looked tired and sad. She went out to take some plants to the woman next door. While she was out Father came in from the garden suddenly.

"Do you know what?" he said to Toby and Claire. "I have just remembered something. It is your mother's birthday today and we have forgotten all about it. That is what comes of having a witch in the house. We must go and buy birthday presents at once."

"But it's Sunday, Daddy!" cried Claire. "All the shops will be shut!"

"What on earth shall we do?" asked Father. "There must be some way of getting a present for her."

"A present!" said a voice. "Who wants a present?" It was Aunt Nasty with her suitcase, a broomstick and a big black cat at her heels.

"Oh, look at the cat!" cried Claire. "I did not know you had a cat, Aunt Nasty."

"He sits round my neck when we ride in the bus or the plane," said Aunt Nasty proudly. "It is his own idea, and it is a good one, because people think he is a fur collar and I do not have to buy a ticket for him. But what is this I hear? Have you really forgotten to get your mother a birthday present?"

"I'm afraid we have!" said Father sadly.

"Ha!" said Aunt Nasty fiercely. "Now I never ever forgot my mother's birthday. I always had some little gift for her. Once I gave her the biggest blackest rat you ever saw. It was a fine rat and I would have liked it for my own pet, but nothing was too good for my mother. I let her have it."

"I don't think Mummy would like a rat," said Claire.

"I wasn't going to give her one!" snapped Aunt Nasty. "Tell me, can you children draw?"

"Yes," said Toby and Claire.

"Can you draw a birthday cake, jellies, little cakes, sandwiches, roast chickens, bottles of fizzy lemonade, balloons, crackers, pretty flowers, birds and butterflies... and presents too?"

"Yes!" said Toby and Claire.

"Well then, you draw them," said Aunt Nasty, "And I will cook up some magic. Where is the stove? Hmmm! I see it is an electric stove. It is a bit on the clean side, isn't it? An old black stove is of much more use to a witch. Mind you I've got no use for the witch who can't make do with what she can get. I will work something out, you see if I don't."

Claire drew and Toby drew. They covered lots and lots of pages with drawings of cakes and balloons and presents wrapped in pretty paper.

Aunt Nasty came in with a smoking saucepan. "Give me your drawings," she said. "Hurry up, I haven't got all day. Hmmmm! They aren't very good, are they? But they'll have to do. A good witch can manage with a scribble if she has to."

She popped the drawings into the saucepan where they immediately caught fire and burned up to ashes. A thick blue smoke filled the room. No one could see anyone else.

"This smoke tastes like birthday cake," called Claire.

"It tastes like jelly and ice-cream," said Toby. The smoke began to go away up the chimney.

"I smell flowers," said Father.

Then they saw that the whole room was changed.

Everywhere there were leaves and flowers and birds only as big as your little finger-nail. The table was covered with jellies of all colours, and little cakes and sandwiches. There was a trifle and two roasted chickens. There were huge wooden dishes of fruit – even grapes, cherries and pineapples. There was a big silver bowl of fizzy lemonade with rose petals floating in it. All around the table were presents and crackers and balloons – so many of them they would have come up to your knees.

"Aha!" said Aunt Nasty, looking pleased. "I haven't lost my touch with a bit of pretty magic."

Best of all was the birthday cake. It was so big there was no room for it on the table. It stood like a pink and white mountain by the fireplace. The balloons bounced and floated around the room. The tiny birds flew everywhere singing. One of them made a nest as small as a thimble in a vase of flowers.

"What is in this parcel?" asked Claire, pointing to a parcel that moved and rustled. "Is it a rat?"

"It's two pigeons," said Aunt Nasty. "There is a pigeon house for them in one of the other parcels. Well, I must be off. I've wasted enough time. The saucepan is spoilt by the way, but you won't mind that. It was a nasty cheap one anyhow."

"Won't you stay and wish Mummy a happy birthday?" asked Toby. "She would like to say thank you for her birthday party."

"Certainly not!" said Aunt Nasty. "I never ever say thank you myself. I don't expect anyone to say it to me. I love rudeness, but that is because I am a witch. You are not witches, so make sure you are polite to everybody." She tied her suitcase to her broomstick with string and her cat climbed onto her shoulder.

"Goodbye to you anyway," she said. "I don't like children, but you are better than most. Perhaps I will see you again or perhaps I won't." She got on her broomstick and flew out of the window, her suitcase bobbing behind her. She was a bit wobbly.

"Well," said Father, "she wasn't so bad after all. It will be strange not having a witch in the house any more."

"Mother will love her birthday," said Claire. "It was good of Aunt Nasty. It is the prettiest party I have ever seen."

"I don't even mind if she visits us again next year," said Toby.

"Look, there is Mummy coming now," said Father. "Let's go and meet her."

They all ran out into the sunshine shouting "Happy Birthday!" Toby had a quick look up in the air for Aunt Nasty. There far above him he saw a tiny little black speck that might have been Aunt Nasty or it might have been a seagull. He was not quite sure. Then he took one of Mother's hands, and Claire took the other, and they pulled her, laughing and happy, up the steps into her birthday room.

THE GARDEN'S FULL OF WITCHES

Mum! The garden's full of witches!
Come quick and see the witches.
    There's a full moon out,
    And they're flying about,
Come on! You'll miss the witches.

Oh Mum! You're missing the witches.
You have never seen so many witches.
    They are casting spells!
    There are horrible smells!
Come on! You'll miss the witches.

Mum, hurry! Come look at the witches.
The shrubbery's bursting with witches.
    They've turned our Joan
    Into a garden gnome.
Come on! You'll miss the witches.

Oh no! You'll miss the witches.
The garden's black with witches.
    Come on! Come on!
    Too late! They've gone.
Oh, you always miss the witches!

Colin McNaughton

DANCE TO YOUR DADDY

Dance to your daddy, my little laddie,
Dance to your daddy, my little man.
You shall have a fishie on a little dishie,
You shall have a fishie
When the boat comes in.

Traditional, Northumberland

BROWN SKIN GIRL

Brown Skin Girl, stay home and mind baby,
Brown Skin Girl, stay home and mind baby,
I'm going away on a fishing boat
And if I don't come back, stay home
and mind baby.

Caribbean

BOBBY SHAFTOE

Bobby Shaftoe's gone to sea,
Silver buckles on his knee,
He'll come back and marry me,
Bonny Bobby Shaftoe.

Bobby Shaftoe's gettin' a bairn,
For to dangle on his arm,
On his arm and on his knee,
Bonny Bobby Shaftoe.

Bobby Shaftoe's bright and fair,
Combing out his yellow hair,
He'll be mine for ever mair,
Bonny Bobby Shaftoe.

Traditional English

MILLY-MOLLY-MANDY
GETS A SURPRISE

from THE MILLY-MOLLY-MANDY OMNIBUS
by Joyce Lankester Brisley

Once upon a time, after morning school, Milly-Molly-Mandy saw Mrs
Green (the lady who lived in the Big House with the iron railings, which
wasn't far from the school) just getting out of her motor-car; and her little
girl Jessamine was with her.

And when the little girl Jessamine saw Milly-Molly-Mandy she said,
"Hullo, Milly-Molly-Mandy! We've just come back from the town.
Mother's been to the hairdresser's and had her hair cut off!"

So when Milly-Molly-Mandy got home to the nice white cottage with
the thatched roof, and was having dinner with Father and Mother and
Grandpa and Grandma and Uncle and Aunty, she told them the news.
And Mother and Grandma and Aunty were quite interested. Mother felt
her 'bun', and said, "I wonder what I should look like with my hair
short!"

Father said, "I like you best as you are."

And Grandpa said, "Nonsense, Polly!"

And Grandma said, "You'd always have to be going to the barber's."

And Uncle said, "You'll be wanting us to have our beards bobbed next!"

And Aunty said, "It wouldn't suit you!"

But Milly-Molly-Mandy said, "Oh, *do*, Mother! Just like me! And then you'd look like my sister!" She looked at Mother carefully, trying to see her with short hair, and added, "I think you'd make a nice sister. DO, Mother!"

Mother laughed and said, "Oh, it wants a lot of thinking about, Milly-Molly-Mandy!"

The next evening Mother took a new cream cheese down the road to the Moggs's cottage, and Milly-Molly-Mandy ran with her. And when Mother had given the cream cheese to Mrs Moggs she said, "Mrs Moggs, what do you think about my having my hair off?"

And when Mrs Moggs had thanked Mother for the cream cheese she said, "Never! It would be a shame to cut your hair off. I wonder how it would suit me!"

Mother said, "Let's go and have it done together!" And Milly-Molly-Mandy said, "Yes, do!" But Mrs Moggs wouldn't.

It was very windy, and going back up the road again Mother lost her comb, and they couldn't find it as it was getting dark and it was probably in among the grasses under the hedge. So Mother went indoors with her hair quite untidy, and she said, "Now, if I had short hair that would not have happened!"

But Father said again, "You're much nicer as you are."

And Grandpa said again, "Nonsense, Polly, you, the mother of a big girl like Milly-Molly-Mandy!"

But Grandma said, "It would be very comfortable."

And Uncle said, "You can always grow it again if you want to!"

And Aunty said, "Well, it wouldn't suit ME!"

Mother's eyebrows said, "Shall I?" to Milly-Molly-Mandy, and Milly-Molly-Mandy's head said, "Yes!" quite decidedly.

The next day Father said he had to drive into the town to buy some gardening tools which he couldn't get at Mr Blunt's shop in the village; and Mother said she would like to go too. (Milly-Molly-Mandy thought Father and Mother had a sort of smiley look, almost as if they had a little secret between them.)

So Father and Mother drove off in the pony-trap together. And when Milly-Molly-Mandy was walking home from school that afternoon with little-friend-Susan she suddenly began to wonder if Mother was going to have her hair cut off in the town, like the little girl Jessamine's mother did.

And she was in such a hurry to get home and see if Mother had come back that as soon as they came to the Moggs's cottage she said "Good-bye" at once to little-friend-Susan, without stopping to look in at her baby sister, or stand and talk or anything, and ran all the rest of the way home.

And when she got into the kitchen there was Mother sitting by the fire making toast for tea; and Grandma and Aunty were looking at her in an amused sort of way all the time they were putting cups on the table or buttering the toast.

For Mother's hair was short like Milly-Molly-Mandy's; and she looked so nice, and yet quite motherly still, that Milly-Molly-Mandy was as pleased as pleased!

"Has Father seen you?" she asked. And Mother and Grandma and Aunty all laughed and said, "Yes."

Milly-Molly-Mandy wondered why they laughed quite like that.

Then Mother said, "Ring the bell outside the back door, Milly-Molly-Mandy, to tell the men-folk tea is ready." So Milly-Molly-Mandy rang the bell loudly, and she could hear the men-folk's voices round by the barn. She wondered what they were laughing at.

Then everybody sat down to tea, and Milly-Molly-Mandy couldn't keep her eyes off Mother's hair. Mother looked so nice, and sort of smiley; Milly-Molly-Mandy couldn't think what she was smiling at so, as she put sugar in the cups. Uncle looked sort of smiley, too, down in his beard – everybody was looking sort of smiley!

Milly-Molly-Mandy looked round the table in surprise.

And then she saw there was a strange man sitting in Father's place! And she was so surprised that she stared hard, while everybody watched her and laughed outright.

And then Mother patted her shoulder, and said, "Wasn't Father naughty? He went and had his beard cut off while I was having my hair done!"

And the 'strange man' who was Father stroked his chin, and said, "Don't you think I look very nice shingled too, Milly-Molly-Mandy?"

It was quite a long time before Milly-Molly-Mandy was able to say anything. And then she wanted to know what Father and Mother thought of each other.

And Father said, "I told you before, I like her best just as she is – so I do!"

And Mother said, "I'll like him best as he is – when I get used to it!"

And when Milly-Molly-Mandy had tried how it felt kissing Father without his beard she said in a satisfied way, "I think everybody's nicest as they are, really, aren't they?"

And Aunty, poking a hairpin back in her own hair, quite agreed.

BIRTHDAY

Tomorrow there are going to be:
Hugs and kisses,
cards in the post,
balloons, probably,
a big cake with icing
and candles,
chocolate biscuits,
and crisps,
ice cream,
and lots of presents.
Alfie's friends are all coming tomorrow,
and they'll have to be
especially nice to him
because it's going to be
Alfie's birthday!

Shirley Hughes

TOD AND THE BIRTHDAY PRESENT

from HERE COMES TOD
by Philippa Pearce

Tod had had a birthday, with birthday cards and birthday presents, and a party with a birthday cake with candles, and party games afterwards.

"What a birthday!" said his father at the end of the day. He was putting Tod to bed, while Tod's mother finished the clearing up downstairs. Tod was in the bath and his father was washing his back for him. "And remember, Tod," said his father, "another birthday very soon!"

"No," said Tod. "I only have one birthday a year, that's all. I know that; and you're just being silly."

"Not your birthday," his father said. "It's your mum who'll be having the birthday."

"Oh," said Tod. He took the sponge from his father and washed his knees while he thought. "Are you giving her a birthday present?"

"Of course," said his father. "I've bought it already. It's a silk scarf of the colours she likes. There's a lot of blue in it to go with the colour of her eyes."

"Is Granny giving her a present?"

"Yes, a pair of warm gloves."

Tod stood up in the bath. He was quite clean by now. He said, "I want to give her something special. I'll buy her that helicopter in the toy shop window."

"Do you think she'd really like that?"

"I would. That helicopter would be my best thing."

"She's different, Tod."

Tod thought, while his father towelled him dry. "All right, then. Not the helicopter," he said. "But I want to give her something really, really special. I'll have to think."

"You do that," said his father. "And remember, Tod: most of all she'd like to be given something you've made for her."

"I'll remember," said Tod.

All the next day, on and off, Tod thought, and then he asked his father, "Could you teach me how to knit?"

"I think so," said his father. "But why?"

"I could knit something for her birthday present. A little mat in blue wool, to go with the colour of her eyes."

So Tod's father looked out some blue wool in the wool bag, and a pair of knitting-needles, and he began to teach Tod to knit. It was very difficult. In the middle of Tod's lesson, his mother walked into the room. She asked at once, "What are you two doing with my knitting-needles? And isn't that my wool?"

"Yes," said Tod's father. "But it's all right. I'm just teaching Tod to knit. He needs to knit something special."

At that Tod threw the knitting-needles and the wool down on the floor and shouted at his father, "Now you've spoilt everything! It won't be a surprise!"

His father began to apologise; and his mother said quickly, "Tod, I didn't see properly what you were doing, and I didn't hear properly what was said. I don't know anything."

"Yes, you do," said Tod. "You're just pretending not to know. But I know you know, and you know I know you know. And it's all ruined!"

Tod burst into tears and rushed out of the house and into the garden. He rushed down to the very bottom of the garden, behind the garden shed, where he often went when he was feeling upset or miserable.

He was a long time coming back, but his father waited for him. At last he appeared, walking quite briskly and looking rather pleased with himself. He said, "I found something special down at the bottom of the garden."

"You've not been in my shed?" said his father.

"No," said Tod. "I was just looking down, feeling cross, when I saw something lying on the earth where you'd been digging."

"Well, what was it?"

"It's in my pocket," said Tod, "and I'm not going to tell you what it is or what I'm going to make with it, because you can't keep a secret. It's going to be my surprise for the birthday."

Tod went upstairs into the bathroom and shut the door. Then

Tod's father heard him washing something in the wash-basin. He scrubbed something with the nail-brush, and then he dried something on the bath towel. Then he came out of the bathroom and went into his own bedroom and hid something there.

Then Tod came downstairs and said to his father, "I'll need string."

"There's a ball of string in the kitchen drawer," said his father.

"No," said Tod. "Not ordinary string. Pretty string. Blue string."

"I think we may have to buy some specially in a shop," said Tod's father.

"I have money," said Tod.

The next Saturday Tod and his father went shopping in the nicest shop in town. Tod's father said to the shop lady, "We want to buy some specially pretty string."

"Blue," said Tod.

"I could perhaps be of more assistance," said the shop lady, "if I knew what the string was needed for."

"You'd better have a private talk with my son about that," said Tod's father. "I'll be at the men's socks counter."

Tod's father went quite a long way off to the men's socks counter. Tod could see him there, and he could see Tod, but he was too far off to hear what Tod was saying.

Tod said to the shop lady, "I'm making a birthday present for my mum. It's to be a surprise, so it has to be kept a secret from my dad, because he's such a chatterbox." Tod looked over at his father; but his father was looking at men's socks. Tod brought something out of his pocket and showed it to the shop lady.

"Aha!" said she. "Now I understand why you were thinking of pretty string. But wouldn't ribbon be better – narrow velvet ribbon in a pretty colour?"

"Blue," said Tod, "because her eyes are blue. And velvet ribbon would be good."

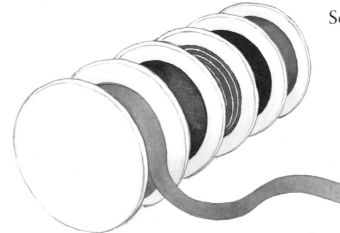

So the shop lady got out a drawer full of velvet ribbons of different widths and colours. Tod chose the narrowest ribbon of a beautiful blue, and the shop lady advised him of the length he would need. She cut off that length and parcelled it up for him, and he paid for it. Then he went off to the men's socks counter and told his father that he was ready to go home.

On the way home, Tod said, "All I need now is an empty matchbox for my present to go into."

"Will it be small enough for a matchbox?" Tod's father asked in astonishment.

"I've just said," said Tod.

When they got home, Tod's father couldn't find an empty matchbox, but he did find two boxes only partly full of matches. Tod saw what must be done. He emptied all the matches from one box into the other, so that one box was full of matches and the other was quite empty. In the middle of his doing this, Tod's mother walked in. "Whatever are you two doing with the matches?" she asked.

"Just rearranging them in their boxes," said Tod's father; and Tod quietly said to him, "Well done!"

Tod's mother didn't ask any more questions.

That evening Tod stuck white paper all over the empty matchbox. Then he decorated it with pink and blue crayons. He drew a little picture of himself on top with a balloon coming out of his mouth.

Inside the balloon he got his father to write:

HAPPY BIRTHDAY!

The next day was the birthday. Everyone was ready for it, and Tod's granny came for the whole day and to spend the night.

At breakfast time, Tod's mother's birthday presents were arranged round her plate. First of all she opened the parcel that had the silk scarf in it. "It's just what I wanted!" she said to Tod's father. "Thank you!"

Then she opened Tod's granny's parcel with the warm gloves inside. "Just what I wanted!" she said to Tod's granny. "Thank you!"

Then she came to the matchbox. "Whatever is this?" she wondered; and Tod's father and his granny both said, "Whatever is it?"

Tod's mother opened the matchbox. "Oh!" she cried in amazement. She lifted out of the matchbox a narrow blue velvet ribbon with its two ends tied firmly together. Dangling from the ribbon was a small, unusual-shaped stone. The stone was a pretty, light brown with white markings. What made the stone so unusual was a hole that went right through the middle of it. The blue velvet ribbon went through that hole.

"Oh!" said Tod's mother again. "It's to hang round my neck." And she hung it round her neck. "It's a pendant."

"Yes," said Tod. "That's exactly what it is. Not a necklace; a pendant. That's what the shop lady said it would be."

"It's so pretty!" said Tod's mother. "The velvet ribbon – "

"Blue," said Tod. "To go with the colour of your eyes."

"– And the stone is so pretty and so very, very unusual, with a hole right through the middle of it. Wherever did you find such a stone, Tod?"

"Just in the garden," said Tod. "I wasn't even looking for it. But, as soon as I saw it, I thought I could make something really special for your birthday."

"And so you did!" said his mother. "Thank you, Tod! Thank you!"

Tod's mother wore her pendant all day. In the evening, Tod's father was going to take her out for a birthday treat; and, while they were out, Tod's granny would look after him.

Tod was in bed and his granny was just going to read him his bedtime story, when Tod's mother came in to say good-night. She was already dressed for going out; she had her coat on, and her birthday scarf and her birthday gloves. As she bent over to kiss Tod, something swung forward from between the folds of the scarf and knocked gently against Tod's face: the pendant. Tod put up his hand and took the brown and white stone between his fingers.

"Do you really like it?" he asked.

"Very, very much."

"But you never said it was just what you wanted."

"How could I, Tod? I couldn't have wanted such a thing, because I couldn't possibly have imagined that such a thing existed: a beautiful stone with a hole through it, found in our very own garden and made by you into a pendant, just for me! It still amazes me, and it's one of the loveliest presents I've ever had."

"Good," said Tod.

When Tod heard the front door close behind his mother and father, he said to his granny, "She's having a specially nice birthday, isn't she? And now you can start reading to me, please."

Please

Please

Please

Please

Please

Please

SAY PLEASE

I'll have a please sandwich cheese
No I mean a knees sandwich please
Sorry I mean a fleas sandwich please
No a please sandwich please
No   No –
I'll have a doughnut.

Michael Rosen

AMELIARANNE AND THE GREEN UMBRELLA

by Constance Heward

Her name was Ameliaranne Stiggins. She was a pale child with black hair, which she wore in curl rags from Friday night till Sunday morning.

Her mother was poor and took in washing. Because, besides Ameliaranne, who was the eldest, there were five other little Stigginses to feed.

Now, it happened one day just before Christmas that the five little Stigginses had colds in their heads, so Mrs Stiggins sat them in a ring in the kitchen with their feet in the middle in a tub of mustard and water.

After that she put them into the big bed and gave them hot gruel to drink; while Ameliaranne stood gloomily by and shook her head, which was covered with curl rags. The reason for the curl rags was that all the village children had been invited to a grand tea-party at the Squire's the next day; and Ameliaranne was gloomy because it did not seem as if the five little Stigginses would be able to go.

Sure enough the next day the colds were worse, and at three o'clock in the afternoon Ameliaranne's hair was taken out of the rags, and she put on her Sunday dress and coat and hat, and started off to the tea-party with twenty-five ringlets bobbing about round her neck.

And the five little Stigginses sat up in the big bed and howled horribly with disappointment.

But Ameliaranne had hardly got out of the front door before she was back again. "I want the umbrella," she said, and she took it from the corner in the parlour where it lived. It was large and green, with a goose's head for a handle.

"It's never going to rain, Ameliaranne," said Mrs Stiggins. "Whatever do you want to take the umbrella for I don't know." But Ameliaranne tossed her head and said she wasn't so sure about the rain, and she started off again with the green umbrella clasped in one hand.

The Squire was a jolly old man with a round red face and a white beard like Father Christmas.

But the Squire's sister, Miss Josephine, was a cross old maid, and she thought it was a stupid thing to give a tea-party to the village children. She was always there to see that they behaved themselves.

Now Miss Josephine's eagle eye was upon Ameliaranne as she took her seat at the great long table with the other children, and – "AMELIYA ANNE STIGGINS!" she said, "what are you doing with that great umbrella in here? You ought to have left it in the hall with your coat and hat."

"Oh, nothing, please, mum," stammered Ameliaranne, turning as red as a boiled lobster and trying to hide the umbrella under the table; and Miss Josephine stared very hard at her and then went on to find fault with somebody else.

What a tea that was! There were cakes with pink icing and cherries on the top, and jam tarts that melted in one's mouth, and biscuits with creamy insides, and scones, and buns.

Ameliaranne seemed to be terribly hungry, for her plate was nearly always empty; but, though she did not reach out and help herself, she was never allowed to wait long, because there were a great many smiling maids to pass the cakes and fill up the tea-cups.

When tea was over the children went back to the hall and put on their hats and coats, and as they went out a smart footman at the door gave each child an orange, an apple, and a bag of sweets.

Ameliaranne was the last to leave, because her hat had fallen down off the peg where she had hung it and was only found after all the other children had gone.

She took her orange and apple and bag of sweets from the smart footman and said, "Thank you, sir," and was just ready to go out through the door, when suddenly Miss Josephine stepped forward.

"AMELIYA ANNE STIGGINS!" she said. "I will put up your umbrella for you," and she took it firmly out of Ameliaranne's hand.

"Oh, mum!" cried Ameliaranne, and the orange and apple and bag of sweets fell down and rolled away under the chairs, and she clutched Miss Josephine's arm in both hands.

But Miss Josephine shook her off and held up the umbrella and fairly shot it open, and out upon the floor, in the bright light that came from the hall lamp, fell jam tarts and iced cakes and biscuits and scones.

And Ameliaranne covered her face with her hands and wept.

"GREEDY CHILD!" said Miss Josephine, but the Squire looked down at the feast on the floor and patted Ameliaranne kindly on the shoulder.

"Come, come!" he said. "It was *your own tea* you put into the umbrella. I know, because I was watching you, and you never ate anything at all."

"Oh, sir," cried Ameliaranne, uncovering her face, "I'm glad you saw, 'cos I didn't take a bit more'n what I could easy 'ave ate; and the five of them's got colds in their 'eads, and when I left them they was all howlin' somethink horful, and I couldn't bear to go home and tell them everything and them not 'ave a bite, as you might say."

"Well, well!" said the Squire, "I thought there was somebody missing, and of course there'll be five teas left over, and I think we could find a sixth as this one is spoilt. John," to the smart footman, "a basket, please, with cakes for six people," and John went like a shot, while Miss Josephine dropped the umbrella and walked slowly past Ameliaranne and the Squire with her nose in the air and a look of horrified disgust on her face.

In two minutes John was back again with a huge basket covered with a white cloth, and fifteen minutes later Ameliaranne staggered into the Stiggins's house and upstairs to the bedroom, with the huge basket on one arm and the green umbrella clutched in the other.

And the five little Stigginses sat up in bed with their eyes nearly starting out of their heads, and Mrs Stiggins sat bump upon a chair because she said it gave her quite a turn when Ameliaranne took the cover off the basket.

For inside that basket were cakes enough for six and Mrs Stiggins as well; and oranges and apples and bags of sweets; and when everybody had finished Ameliaranne was sure that she must have eaten quite twice as much as she had meant to bring home in the green umbrella.

THE TUMMY BEAST

One afternoon I said to mummy,
"Who is this person in my tummy?
"He must be small and very thin
"Or how could he have gotten in?"
My mother said from where she sat,
"It isn't nice to talk like that."
"It's true!" I cried. "I swear it, mummy!
"There *is* a person in my tummy!
"He talks to me at night in bed,
"He's always asking to be fed,
"Throughout the day, he screams at me,
"Demanding sugar buns for tea.
"He tells me it is not a sin
"To go and raid the biscuit tin.
"I know quite well it's awfully wrong
"To guzzle food the whole day long,
"But really I can't help it, mummy,
"Not with this person in my tummy."
"You horrid child!" my mother cried.
"Admit it right away, you've lied!
"You're simply trying to produce
"A silly asinine excuse!
"*You* are the greedy guzzling brat!
"And that is why you're always fat!"
I tried once more, "*Believe me*, mummy,
"There *is* a person in my tummy."

"I've had enough!" my mother said,
"You'd better go at once to bed!"
Just then, a nicely timed event
Delivered me from punishment.
Deep in my tummy something stirred,
And then an awful noise was heard,
A snorting grumbling grunting sound
That made my tummy jump around.
My darling mother nearly died,
"My goodness, what was that?" she cried.
At once, the tummy voice came through,
It shouted, "Hey there! Listen you!
"I'm getting hungry! I want eats!
"I want lots of chocs and sweets!
"Get me half a pound of nuts!
"Look snappy or I'll twist your guts!"
"*That's him!*" I cried. "*He's in my tummy!*
"So now do you believe me, mummy?"

But mummy answered nothing more,
For she had fainted on the floor.

Roald Dahl

POOR MONTY

by Anne Fine

Monty's mother was a doctor.

A very busy doctor.

She spent her mornings at the surgery.

She spent her lunch times driving round seeing the old folk.

And she spent her afternoons filling in forms.

By the time she came home, all she wanted was to put her feet up and have a cup of tea and a quiet little read of the paper.

Monty tried talking to her. "*Suppose*," he said, "suppose you felt funny all over and a little bit shivery..."

"Mmmm," said his mother, turning over a page.

"And *suppose*," said Monty, "suppose your forehead was hot...

"And suppose your head felt as if little men in steel boots were stamping in it...

"And suppose your tummy felt as if people had made you eat worms..."

"Mmmm," said his mother, turning another page.

"And suppose," bellowed Monty, "suppose when you lifted up your shirt you found you had little red spots all over your body!"

And he burst into tears.

Monty's mother scooped him up and cuddled him.

"Oh, poor Monty!" she said. "What a terrible doctor I am! You've got chicken-pox!"

And Monty felt a little better already.

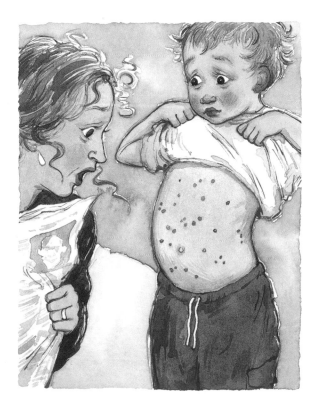

A big storm blew up over our part of the land; the biggest storm that any of us could remember, so big that we thought the Flood had come again. The sky was as black as night all day long, and the wind blew so hard that it drove a strong man backwards, and the rain poured down so that you only had to hold a pitcher out of the window for a second, and when you took it in it was flowing over, and the thunder growled and crackled so that we had to make signs to each other, for talking was no use, and the lightning flashed so bright that my mother could thread her needle by it. That *was* a storm, that was! My mother was frightened, but my father who was weather-wise, watched the sky and said from time to time, "I think that'll come out all right." And so it did. The lightning and thunder flashed and rolled themselves away into the distance, the rain stopped, the wind died down, the sky cleared up for a beautiful evening, and the sun turned all the vast wet sands to a sheet of gold as far as the eye could see. Yes, and farther! For a wonder had happened during the storm. The

sea had been driven back so far that it had vanished out of sight, and sands were laid bare that no living man or woman had viewed before. And there, far, far across the golden beach, lay a tiny village, shining in the setting sun.

Think of our excitement, Mary Matilda! It was the drowned village of long ago, come back to the light of day.

Everybody gathered on the shore to look at it. And suddenly I began to run towards it, and all the other children followed me. At first our parents called, "Come back! come back! the sea may come rolling in before you can get there." But we were too eager to see the village for ourselves, and in the end the big folk felt the same about it; and they came running after the children across the sands. As we drew nearer, the little houses became plainer, looking like blocks of gold in the evening light; and the little streets appeared like golden brooks, and the church spire in the middle was like a point of fire.

For all my little legs, I was the first to reach the village. I had had a start of the others, and could always run fast as a child and never tire. We had long stopped running, of course, for the village was so far out that our breath would not last. But I was still walking rapidly when I reached the village and turned a corner. As I did so, I heard one of the big folk cry, "Oh, look! yonder lies the sea." I glanced ahead, and did see, on the far horizon beyond the village, the shining line of the sea that had gone so far away. Then I heard another grown-up cry, "Take care! take care! Who knows when it may begin to roll back again? We have come far, and oh, suppose the sea should overtake us before we can reach home!" Then, peeping round my corner, I saw everybody take fright and turn tail, running as hard as they could across the mile or so of sands they had just crossed. But nobody had noticed me, or thought of me; no doubt my own parents thought I was one of the band of running children, and so they left me alone there, with all the little village to myself.

What a lovely time I had, going into the houses, up and down the streets, and through the church. Everything was left as it had been, and seemed ready for someone to come to; the flowers were blooming in the gardens, the fruit was hanging on the trees, the tables were spread for the next meal, a pot was standing by the kettle on the hearth in one house,

and in another there were toys upon the floor. And when I began to go upstairs to the other rooms, I found in every bed someone asleep. Grandmothers and grandfathers, mothers and fathers, young men and young women, boys and girls: all so fast asleep, that there was no waking them. And at last, in a little room at the top of a house, I found a baby in a cradle, wide awake.

She was the sweetest baby I had ever seen. Her eyes were as blue as the sea that had covered them so long, her skin as white as the foam, and her little round head as gold as the sands in the evening sunlight. When she saw me, she sat up in her cradle, and crowed with delight. I knelt down beside her, held out my arms, and she cuddled into them with a little gleeful chuckle. I carried her about the room, dancing her up and down in my arms, calling her my baby, my pretty Sea-Baby, and showing her the things in the room and out of the window. But as we were looking out of the window at a bird's nest in a tree, I seemed to see the shining line of water on the horizon begin to move.

"The sea is coming in!" I thought. "I must hurry back before it catches us." And I flew out of the house with the Sea-Baby in my arms, and ran as hard as I could out of the village, and followed the crowd of golden footsteps on the sands, anxious to get home soon. When I had to pause to get my breath, I ventured to glance over my shoulder, and there behind me lay the little village, still glinting in the sun. On I ran again, and after a while was forced to stop a second time. Once more I glanced behind me, and this time the village was not to be seen: it had disappeared beneath the tide of the sea, which was rolling in behind me.

Then how I scampered over the rest of the way! I reached home just as the tiny wavelets, which run in front of the big waves, began to lap my ankles, and I scrambled up the cliff, with the Sea-Baby in my arms, and got indoors, panting for breath. Nobody was at home, for as it happened they were all out looking for me. So I took my baby upstairs, and put her to bed in my own bed, and got her some warm milk. But she turned from the milk, and wouldn't drink it. She only seemed to want to laugh and play with me. So I did for a little while, and then I told her she must go to sleep. But she only laughed some more, and went on playing.

"Shut your eyes, baby," I said to her, "hush-hush! hush-hush!" (just as my own mother said to me). But the baby didn't seem to understand, and went on laughing.

Then I said, "You're a very naughty baby" (as my mother sometimes used to say to me). But she didn't mind that either, and just went on laughing. So in the end I had to laugh too, and play with her.

My mother heard us, when she came into the house; and she ran up to find me, delighted that I was safe. What was her surprise to find the baby with me! She asked me where it had come from, and I told her; and she called my father, and he stood scratching his head, as most men do when they aren't quite sure about a thing.

"I want to keep it for my own, Mother," I said.

"Well, we can't turn it out now it's in," said my mother. "But you'll have to look after it yourself, mind."

I wanted nothing better! I'd always wanted to nurse things, whether it was a log of wood, or a kitten, or my mother's shawl rolled into a dumpy bundle. And now I had a little live baby of my own to nurse. How I did enjoy myself that week! I did everything for it; dressed and undressed it, washed it, and combed its hair; and played and danced with it, and talked with it and walked with it. And I tried to give it its meals, but it wouldn't eat; and I tried to put it to sleep, but it wouldn't shut its eyes. No, not for anything I could do, though I sang to it, and rocked it, and told it little stories.

It didn't worry me much, for I knew no better: but it worried my mother, and I heard her say to my father, "There's something queer about that child. I don't know, I'm sure!"

On the seventh night after the storm, I woke up suddenly from my dreams, as I lay in bed with my baby beside me. It was very late, my

parents had long gone to bed themselves, and what had wakened me I did not know, for I heard no sound at all. The moon was very bright, and filled the square of my window-pane with silver light; and through the air outside I saw something swimming – I thought at first it was a white cloud, but as it reached my open window I saw it was a lady, moving along the air as though she were swimming in water. And the strange thing was that her eyes were fast shut; so that as her white arms moved out and in she seemed to be swimming not only in the air, but in her sleep.

She swam straight through my open window to the bedside, and there she came to rest, letting her feet down upon the floor like a swimmer setting his feet on the sands under his body. The lady leaned over the bed with her shut eyes, and took my wide-awake baby in her arms.

"*Hush-hush! Hush-hush!*" she said; and the sound of her voice was not like my mother's voice when she said it, but like the waves washing the shore on a still night; such a peaceful sound, the sort of sound that might have been the first sound made in the world, or else the last. You couldn't help wanting to sleep as you heard her say it. I felt my head begin to nod, and as it grew heavier and heavier, I noticed that my Sea-Baby's eyelids were beginning to droop too. Before I could see any more, I fell asleep; and when I awoke in the morning, my baby had gone. "Where to, Mary Matilda? Ah, you mustn't ask me that! I only knew she must have gone where all babies go when they go to sleep. Go to sleep. Hush-hush! *Hush-hush! Go to sleep!*"

*

Mary Matilda had gone to sleep at last. The Old Nurse laid her softly in her cot, turned down the light, and crept out of the nursery.

LITTLE FAN

"I don't like the look of little Fan, mother,
   I don't like her looks a little bit.
Her face – well, it's not exactly different,
   But there's something wrong with it.

"She went down to the sea-shore yesterday,
   And she talked to somebody there,
Now she won't do anything but sit
   And comb out her yellowy hair.

"Her eyes are shiny and she sings, mother,
   Like nobody ever sang before.
Perhaps they gave her something queer to eat,
   Down by the rocks on the shore.

"Speak to me, speak, little Fan dear,
  Aren't you feeling very well?
Where have you been and what are you singing,
  And what's that seaweedy smell?

"Where did you get that shiny comb, love,
  And those pretty coral beads so red?
Yesterday you had two legs, I'm certain,
  But now there's something else instead.

"I don't like the looks of little Fan, mother,
  You'd best go and close the door.
Watch now, or she'll be gone for ever
  To the rocks by the brown sandy shore."

James Reeves

LULLABY

Hush you bye, don't you cry,
Go to sleep little baby.
When you wake, you shall have
All the pretty little horses.

Blacks and bays, dapples and greys,
Coach and six little horses.

Hush you bye, don't you cry,
Go to sleep little baby.
When you wake, you'll have sweet cake,
And all the pretty little horses.

A brown and a grey and a black and a bay
And a coach and six little horses.

Hush you bye, don't you cry,
Oh you pretty little baby.
Go to sleep little baby,
Oh you pretty little baby.

Traditional
Southern States of USA

SING LULA BYE-BYE

Sing lula, lula, lula, lula bye-bye
Do you want the moon to play with?
Or the stars to run away with?
They'll come if you don't cry.

Husha lula, lula, lula, lula bye-bye
From your mammy's arms you're peepin'
And soon you'll be a-sleepin'
Husha lula, lula, lula, lula-bye.

Traditional

ACKNOWLEDGEMENTS

The publishers would like to thank the copyright holders for permission to reproduce the following copyright material. Every effort has been made to trace the ownership of all copyrighted material and to secure the necessary permission to reprint these selections. In the event of any question arising as to the use of any material, the editor and publisher, while expressing regret for any inadvertent error, will be happy to make the necessary correction in future printings.

Master Salt the Sailor's Son by Allan Ahlberg, (Penguin Group), text © Allan Ahlberg, 1980, reproduced by permission of Penguin UK • 'The Little Girl and the Tiny Doll' by Aingelda and Edward Ardizzone, from *Stories for Under-Fives* (Longman Young Books), © Aingelda and Edward Ardizzone 1966, reproduced by permission of Laura Cecil Literary Agency • 'Milly-Molly-Mandy Gets a Surprise' from *More of Milly-Molly-Mandy*, (first published by George G Harrap, 1929), text copyright © Joyce Lankester Brisley, reproduced by permission of Larousse plc • 'The Tummy Beast' by Roald Dahl, from *Dirty Beasts* (Jonathan Cape), reproduced by permission of David Higham Associates• 'The Special Offer Pens' from *Joe and Timothy Together* by Dorothy Edwards, (Methuen Children's Books, 1971), reproduced by permission of Reed Consumer Books Ltd • 'The Sea-Baby' from *The Old Nurse's Stocking Basket* by Eleanor Farjeon (Michael Joseph), reproduced by permission of David Higham Associates • *Poor Monty* by Anne Fine, (Methuen Children's Books, 1992), reproduced by permission of Reed Consumer Books Ltd • 'Birthday' from *The Big Alfie and Annie Rose Story Book* by Shirley Hughes, (The Bodley Head), reproduced by permission of Random House UK Ltd • *Ameliaranne and the Green Umbrella* (first published by George G Harrap, 1920), text copyright © Constance Heward, reproduced by permission of Larousse plc • 'Aunt Nasty' from *Mahy Magic* by Margaret Mahy, (J.M. Dent), reproduced by permission of The Orion Publishing Group Ltd • 'Bully Boy McCoy' from *Making Friends With Frankenstein* © 1993 Colin McNaughton; 'Monday's Child is Red and Spotty' and 'The Garden's Full of Witches' from *There's an Awful Lot of Weirdo's in our Neighbourhood* © 1987 Colin McNaughton. Reproduced by permission of the publisher Walker Books Ltd • 'Disobedience' from *When We Were Very Young* by A A Milne, (Methuen Children's Books), reproduced by permission of Reed Consumer Books Ltd • 'Tod and the Birthday Present' from *Here Comes Tod* © 1992 Philippa Pearce. Illustrated by Adriano Gon. Reproduced by permission of Walker Books Ltd • 'Say Please' and 'Keith's Cupboard' by Michael Rosen, reproduced by permission of Scholastic Publications Ltd • 'Little Fan' © James Reeves from *Complete Poems for Children*, (Heinemann) by permission of the James Reeves Estate

This edition produced for, The Book People Ltd, Hall Wood Avenue, Haydock, St Helens, WA11 9UL
First published in Great Britain by HarperCollins Publishers Ltd in 1998

1 3 5 7 9 10 8 6 4 2
ISBN: 0 583 33707-4

Compilation copyright © Shirley Hughes 1998
Illustrations copyright © Clara Vulliamy 1998
Introduction © Shirley Hughes 1998
The compiler and illustrator assert the moral right to be identified as the compiler and illustrator of the work.
A CIP catalogue record for this title is available from the British Library.

Printed and bound in Singapore by Tien Wah Press.